M000250639

THE DANIEL FAST

21 Day Food & Faith Journal

CHEF ASHLEY SHEP

THE DANIEL FAST 21 DAY
FOOD AND FAITH JOURNAL

Copyright © 2020 by Simplify Meal Time Publishing

Written by Chef Ashley Shep

For meal plans, products and resources focused on simplifying meal time™, visit www.ChefAshleyShep.com.

INTRODUCTION

Congratulations! You've made the first step towards a deeper relationship with Christ through prayer and fasting. This journal will help you focus on the real reason behind fasting and how you can make this your most successful fast yet. Whether this is your first time fasting or your hundredth, be intentional about your time with God. He's guaranteed to meet you where you are and in a mighty way. Whether you're using this journal as a part of The Daniel Fast 21 Day Food and Faith Challenge, fasting solo or joining your church, my prayer is that it blesses you to stay motivated and on track with your goal of successfully completing the fast.

As a personal chef and meal time strategist, I work with families who are stressed and overwhelmed when it comes to dinnertime. Figuring out what to eat on a regular day takes up time and energy that you can't afford to waste while you're fasting. If you let it, thinking about what to eat can consume your thoughts, and that's definitely not what God wants you to get out of the fast. That's why you'll find over three weeks worth of recipes, meal plans, and much more on the Daniel Fast Extras page at www. ChefAshleyShep.com/DanielFastExtras.

This journal came about because one of my church members was really struggling with what she was going to eat on an upcoming Daniel Fast. Instantly I thought, "I can help with that. I got you sis!" From there came the Daniel Fast 21 Day Food and Faith Challenge and the realization that food could be my ministry. Through the creation of the challenge, I saw how lives were changed by the daily devotionals, encouragement, and the easy to follow recipes. Folks were able to focus on the fast instead of the food (which is the point of the fast in the first place).

So What is the Daniel Fast?

The Daniel Fast is a 21 day shift in dietary and prayer habits that aims to provide a clearer way to hear from God. The modern day version of the fast is inspired by Daniel in the Bible during a time where he "ate no pleasant bread. No meat or wine came into the mouth. I didn't anoint myself at all, until three whole weeks were fullfilled" (Daniel 10:2-3 World English Bible). Other translations have slighlty different wordings of what he didn't consume, but most folks who do The Daniel Fast avoid meat, dairy, other animal by products, and processed foods.

In the United States, the fast is often done at the top of the year around the time of resolutions as a way to set intentions for the year ahead. However, you can do the fast any time of the year when you need a spiritual reset to draw closer to God. At first glance, the fast seems to be mostly about food, but it's actually about stretching your faith in God through prayer. It's an outward sacrifice for inward growth.

During this time, my prayer is that you:

1. Gain a deeper connection with our Lord and Savior.
2. Find more time to focus on Him.
3. Spend less time figuring out what to eat.

Just like the Holy Trinity, I've found that the trifecta

below makes the perfect combination to help you successfully complete the Daniel Fast:

1. Daily Devotionals: To keep you uplifted and focused on why you're fasting
2. Community: To stay encouraged along with others by joining the Daniel Fast with Chef Ashley Shep private Facebook group
3. Recipes & Meal Planner: To keep you on track and know what in the world you're eating.

So now you might be wondering, "Where Do I Begin?"

- Write down what you're believing in God for during the fast.
- Visit www.ChefAshleyShep.com/DanielFastExtras to get access to Daniel Fast approved recipes, the private Facebook group, and other helpful links that I'll mention throughout this book.
- Use the meal planner sheets to map out your meals for the week.

HOW TO
USE THIS
__ JOURNAL __

At The Start of The Fast

Pray about and select a few things that God has placed on your heart to have faith for during the fast. This could be for yourself or for others. Get familiar with the contents of this journal so you'll be ready to use it when your fast starts.

Each Day

Pick a time of day that works for you to complete reading your devotionals and journal about your thoughts and prayers. Keep track of your meals and snacks as well as your feelings about food. Since it's only you and God listening, be honest. He already knows what you're thinking anyway.

Each Week

Reflect upon how the previous week went and set your intentions for the upcoming one. That means, pick which meals you're going to eat and decide where you're looking for God to show up.

Medical/Spiritual Disclaimers:

First, please realize that this journal isn't the Bible, and I'm not Jesus. In other words:

1.   Check with your doctor before beginning or changing any new fitness or dietary program. This is especially necessary if you have any medical conditions that make fasting/dieting difficult (pregnancy, diabetes, etc.). The information provided here is purely educational and does not represent medical advice and is not intended to diagnose or treat any condition. The content of this journal is not intended to replace any advice that you receive from a medical professional. (You can't do work in the kingdom if you're fallin' out.)

2.   Though this is divinely inspired, God's word and your personal discernment come first. (BUT if your discernment is telling you that it's ok to get waffle fries from the drive thru, just know that ain't God lol.)

3.   Affiliate Disclaimer: For some of the products or services I share with you, I may get a few dollars or cents as a thank you from the company for the recommendation (at no extra cost to you). I don't recommend or endorse any product that I don't use myself or haven't heavily researched. So, if I share it, it's quality. I just wanted to give a heads up and keep it completely 100.

4.   By purchasing this journal, you agree that Chef Ashley Shep LLC and its owner will not be held liable in the event that you are injured, harmed, etc. as a result of any of the information here.

5.   These devotionals started out as emails from my annual Daniel Fast 21 Day Food and Faith Challenge. When I talk to my audience, I speak like I'm talking with a good friend/sister: uplifting, supportive, and sometimes convicting. Plus I'm from the southern United States. So, that being said, know that you'll find a few places that aren't "standard English", because I want to talk to you like you're one of my girlfriends. Additionally, if you're interested in finding out about the challenge, visit www.ChefAshleyShep.com/DanielFastExtras.

6.   Lastly, I'm flawed just like you, so blame any mistakes on my head and not my heart. You can send corrections to help@chefashleyshep.com

FOOD LIST

So What Can I Eat?

All Fruits All Vegetables All Whole Grains All Beans & Legumes All Nuts & Seeds Plant Based Oils Water, 100% Fruit Juices, 100% Vegetable Juices	**You'll want to avoid:** All Animal Products (such as meat, seafood, & honey) All Dairy Products All Heavily Processed Foods (ex. fried foods, added chemicals, bread, etc) All Sweeteners

Be sure to check out the Daniel Fast Extras page for recipe ideas with these foods (www.ChefAshleyShep.com/DanielFastExtras).
If you're unsure about a food, ask yourself these questions:

1. Is this food bringing me closer to or further away from strengthening my faith?
2. Do I think about this food more than I think about God?
3. Do I want this food out of boredom, anxiety, or lack of control about something that's happening in my life?

If all else fails, go to God and ask His thoughts on the food.
Remember, instead of focusing on the food you can't have, focus on the deeper relationship you can have with Christ.

MEAL
PLANNING
TIPS
—   —

My intention during our time together is to not only help you complete the fast, but also provide you with tips that will work, even when you're not fasting. I'm a teacher by nature and trade, so catch the lesson.

Give a man a fish and you feed him one meal. Teach him to fish and he can feed himself for many meals."
- Unknown

So let's go fishing.

Tip #1: Shop/Order Groceries on Saturday or Sunday

Purchase your food on Saturday or Sunday to avoid middle of the week runs to the grocery store and the temptation to get stuff you don't even want or actually need.

Since you're going to be making multiple new recipes, ordering your groceries online could be another good way to save time, cut stress, and leave less chance of you buying something you'll regret later. Plus, you can schedule your order for pick up or delivery up to four days in advance at most stores. (Get my free online grocery shopping comparison chart at www.ChefAshleyShep.com/DanielFastExtras to see different options available near you.)

Tip #2: Use a Meal Planning App/Site

*"Write the vision, and make it plain on tablets, that
he who runs may read it."*
- Habakkuk 2:2 (WEB)

Without vision, the people will perish. Ok, so you're not gonna die if you don't meal plan, but God won't bless mess. Use the meal planner to "write the vision" for your week and "make it plain" that you're committed to honoring God during this time with your meals. If you prefer to plan your meals, then I suggest using a site like Plan to Eat or the Dope
Vegan Meal Planner. Links to both of these sites are available on the Daniel Fast Extras page at
www.ChefAshleyShep.com/DanielFastExtras.

Plan to Eat is a digital storing system for all your recipes so that you're not left trying to remember where that scrap of paper, blog post, or Pin is that had that recipe at one time. You can upload any of your own favorite recipes or add them from any website. From there, you can select your meals for the week and Plan to Eat will make your grocery list for you in minutes. Plus, they have an app that you can use to make sure you never forget another ingredient at the store again.

If you're thinking about switching to eating plant based meals for the long haul, you'll definitely want to try out The Dope Vegan Meal Planner. On this site, you'll have access to hundreds of vegan recipes to choose from to quickly plan out your meals for the week. Culinary creators like myself add recipes to the site for you, so all you have to do is pick what you'd like to eat. The best part of the Dope Vegan Meal Planner is you can order your groceries directly from the site without
having to leave your home.

Both sites help me:

- Save time, energy, & money because I know exactly what I need to buy,
- Store all of my recipes, make sure I don't forget anything, and
- Make it easier to decide what to eat.

If you sign up for Plan to Eat, I'll share my recipes with you there, making it easier for you to add extra snacks or other meals, even when you're not on the fast. Start with their free 30-day trial. If you join the Dope Vegan Meal Planner you'll get your first week free, and my recipes are already available for you to choose from.

But what if you're a pen and paper person?

I've got you covered right here in the journal plus they're additional options on the Daniel Fast Extras page, so be sure to check those out at www.ChefAshleyShep.com/DanielFastExtras.

Today, focus on getting organized so you can fully commit without distractions. When you do, you'll have more energy and more focus on the purpose of the fast: ~~food~~ faith.

WEEK

Meal Planner

Each week, use this sheet to plan out your meals, or record what you ate after each meal. Since you'll need your energy, try to eat breakfast each day. Remember to visit www.ChefAshleyShep.com/DanielFastExtras for recipe ideas from my Daniel Fast Pinterest board and the Facebook group.

USE THE KEY TO RECORD YOUR MEALS:
B - BREAKFAST L - LUNCH D - DINNER S - SNACKS

SUN

B _____

L _____

D _____

S _____

MON

B _____

L _____

D _____

S _____

TUES

B _____

L _____

D _____

S _____

WED

B _____

L _____

D _____

S _____

THURS

B _____

L _____

D _____

S _____

FRI

B _____

L _____

D _____

S _____

SAT

B _____

L _____

D _____

S _____

__ WEEK 1 __

Scriptures to Reflect Upon:

*"Write the vision, and make it plain on tablets,
That he who runs may read it."*
- Habakkuk 2:2 (WEB)

———

*"Where there is no vision, the people perish:
but he that keepeth the law, happy is he."*
- Proverbs 29:18 (KJV)

———

*"Son of man, you dwell in the middle of the
rebellious house, who have eyes to see, and
don't see, who have ears to hear, and don't
hear; for they are a rebellious house."*
- Ezekiel 12:2 (WEB)

———

*"...knowing that the testing of your
faith produces endurance."*
- James 1:3 (WEB)

During the Fast, I'm believing in God for...

FOR MYSELF

_____
_____
_____
_____
_____
_____
_____
_____
_____

FOR OTHERS

_____
_____
_____
_____
_____
_____
_____
_____
_____

Get Your Mind Right
Let's Get Started

Praying and planning out your meals are alike in a few ways.

1. They both bring calmness to your daily life.
2. You're probably not doing either as often as you should be.

> *"It only takes discipline until it becomes a habit."*
>
> - Alston J. Balkcom

3. The more you do it, the more naturally it comes to you.

Now, I'm not saying that praying and figuring out what to eat are of equal importance. What I am saying is, if we know both of these are good for us, we need to think about what's stopping us from doing them.

> *"Where there is no vision, the people perish."*
>
> - Proverbs 29:18 (KJV)

One translation even says when there's no revelation, people are without restraint.

We also need to be intentional about the time we spend doing them. Your prayer life is the way you check in and realign yourself with God and allow Him to order your steps. During this fast, you should find that already having a plan in place for your meals will help your mind focus on more important things like your family, yourself, and your walk with Christ.

Here are some ways
to make time for prayer

- Start in the morning before the craziness of the day begins.
- Consider how your time is spent in the small moments (driving in the car, in the shower, etc.).
- Decide what you can delegate to others to give you more time (grocery shopping, house cleaning, etc. Remember, help isn't that kind of four-letter word.)
- Realize that prayer is just talking to God. That's it.

Making time for meal planning
works in a similar way

- Start thinking of meals you want before you need them. (Monday at 5 after work is too late.)
- Instead of just saving those meals from Facebook or Pinterest, pick 1 or 2 to actually make. (I promise you already have a ton of options.) If not, check out the recipes on the Extras page or my Daniel Fast Pinterest Board (www.ChefAshleyShep.com/DanielFastExtras).
- Let the hubby and/or the kids handle dinner a few nights a month. Even God rested, so why shouldn't you?

I'll be helping with your meals for the next few weeks, so spend some of that extra time setting your intentions for the fast by asking yourself:

- What am I believing in God to do during this fast?
- What events will challenge my strength during this time (birthday cake, office parties, etc.)?
- Is there anything that's holding me back from fully committing?

When you find the answers to these, pray that you will:

- Trust God's word and not yourself. (Proverbs 3:5-6)
- Have eyes to see and ears to hear Him during this time. (Ezekiel 12:2)
- Spend some quiet time today with the Lord to answer the questions on the lines below.

_____

_____

_____

_____

_____

_____

_____

_____

_____

_____

_____

_____

DAY 02

How's Your Heart?

That might seem like a health question since I focus on helping families create healthy meals for their kids. But in this case, it's more of a biblical question.

Let me explain.

> *"For where your treasure is, there your heart will be also."*
>
> - Matthew 6:21 (WEB)

Now, I definitely don't claim to be a Bible scholar, but sometimes I'll read different translations to better understand a verse. When I want a quick word that's easy to understand, then the Common English Bible translation is my go to option. But sometimes when I want to get a little more detail, then I'll switch to the Amplified version. That one reads:

> *"For where your treasure is, there your heart [your wishes, your desires; that on which your life centers] will be also."*
>
> - Matthew 6:21

What does this have to do with food again?

Well, a lot.

Since I first started doing the Daniel Fast 21 Day Food and Faith Challenge, the top question I get is:

"So, what can I eat?"

People want to know what is *"allowed"* and *"not allowed."*

Depending upon which version of Daniel 10:2-3 you read, it says that he didn't eat meat or rich foods. It also says that he didn't anoint himself/put on lotion/bathe. I don't know about you, but I definitely shower at least once a day during the fast.

My point is that you can get caught up in focusing so much on the food and trying to follow things to a T that you miss God. He's more interested in your heart, intention, and follow through.

My job is to make sure you have options that will keep you physically fed to help you focus on being spiritually fed.

Still, at some point during the next few weeks, you're probably going to end up faced with something you're not sure if it's "ok" to eat.

When that happens, just remember Matthew 6:21. And ask yourself:

- Will eating this store up treasures in heaven through my sacrifice?
- Does this honor my sacrifice to God and push me towards strengthening my faith?

If you can answer yes, then gladly enjoy it.

If it's a no for you, then sis, put it down and walk away. Easier said than done I know, but by resisting, you are standing in agreement that your relationship with God is truly far more important than any food on earth.

When we're obedient and reverent, He honors our needs and even our wants. So, take time to honor Him today and thank God for the opportunity to grow closer to Him.

And if you're really unsure as to whether or not something is "approved":
- Check out my What Can I Eat? Pinterest board (www.ChefAshleyShep.com/DanielFastExtras)
- Head to the files section of the Facebook group (www.ChefAshleyShep.com/DanielFastExtras)
- Ask yourself these questions:
  o Did it come from an animal?
  o Does it have added sugar or chemicals I can't pronounce on the label?
  o Was it deep-fried or heavily processed?
- If it's a yes, then it's a no for you.

When you get tempted by food, write here about what your thoughts and feelings are at that moment.

Worth Fighting For

If you've seen "The Color Purple", I'm sure you know the part of the movie where Oprah's character, Sophia, confronts Whoopi Goldberg.

(*Note: In no way am I endorsing or condoning domestic violence. If you or someone you know is a victim, I've added info below to help.)

> While Oprah's talking, she says, "All my life I had to fight."
> This phrase applies to you too.
> All your life you'll have to fight.

Fighting is mentioned many times in the Bible. Even one of Jesus's disciples, Peter, cut off the ear of one of high priest's men when they came to pick up Jesus before the crucifixion. - (Luke 22:51) Jesus healed it up though, so it was all good.

A lot of times when someone starts talking about fighting, people think it means:

- Throwing 'bows (*cue Ludacris*),
- Taking off earrings, and/or
- Using weapons.

Thankfully, you won't need any of those weapons to fight the battles that you'll face during this fast.

Instead, you'll need spiritual weapons.

Check out Ephesians 6:11-17 (CEB) for yourself, and then spend a few minutes to think about how God equips us with all that we need to fight the mental battles that we experience each day (whether we're fasting or not). These verses help when:

- Your laundry is piled high and sink is full,
- You're about to send that "per my last email" email to one of your coworkers who doesn't read anything,
- Your kids don't want to act right, and/or
- You're hangry (hungry + angry).

> *"Put on the whole armor of God, that you may be able to stand against the wiles of the devil. For our wrestling is not against flesh and blood, but against the principalities, against the powers, against the world's rulers of the darkness of this age, and against the spiritual forces of wickedness in the heavenly places. Therefore put on the whole armor of God, that you may be able to withstand in the evil day, and having done all, to stand. Stand therefore, having the utility belt of truth buckled around your waist, and having put on the breastplate of righteousness, and having fitted your feet with the preparation of the Good News of peace, above all, taking up the shield of faith, with which you will be able to quench all the fiery darts of the evil one. And take the helmet of salvation, and the sword of the Spirit, which is the word of God;"*
>
> - Ephesians 6:11-17 (WEB)

He gives us all we need to fight and to win.

How will you fight with God's help during the next few weeks?

_____

_____

_____

_____

_____

_____

_____

_____

_____

_____

_____

_____

_____

_____

_____

_____

*If you or someone you know is experiencing domestic violence, contact the National Domestic Violence Hotline by calling 1-800-799-7233.

It's Not About the Food
Hear me out

> Jesus replied, ***"It's written, people won't live only by bread, but by every word spoken by God."***
>
> - Matthew 4:4 (CEB)

Yeah, I know that sounds crazy, especially coming from me.
Since I'm the one giving you the recipes, and because this is a fast, you're probably most concerned about what you can/can't eat.

But honestly, it's not about the food.

Yeah, I said it. The Daniel Fast ain't about the food. Sure, I'm taking out the guesswork behind the cooking so that you can focus on the point of the fast.
But the food isn't it.

When you have your meals figured out and your grocery list is made, thinking about dinner takes less time each day. It gives you more time to focus on what the fast is really about:

- Coming into alignment with who you are (and want to be) in Christ.
- Placing a demand on your faith.
- Growing your dependence on God and decreasing your dependency on food.

The sacrifice of the food is an outward way to show that what you're standing in faith for is worth more to you than those waffle fries. Or maybe for you it's ice cream... (for me it's both.) There are benefits to honoring God with our minds, bodies, money, and especially our time. Through fasting, I've found:

- My purpose with helping moms lead healthier lives for their families.
- Clarity in direction about decisions (professionally & personally).
- Guidance to accomplish financial blessings (debt pay off/cancellation, unexpected money, etc.).

Even though the fast only lasts 21 days, that's plenty of time for God to turn some things around and set you up for divine acceleration this year.

I'm excited to see and hear your testimonies about how God has changed you after the fast and how the foundation carries you through the rest of the year. Be sure to record your celebrations in today's journaling spot. Today, share one win of how God has made himself known this week. If you'd like to inspire others, be sure to share in the Facebook group as well, so I/we can celebrate with you (www.ChefAshleyShep.com/DanielFastExtras).

What's in a Name?

Jesus is Sweet, and so is almost everything else you're eating.

What do you call God?

For me, He's a peacekeeper, provider, and a jokester at times. When I think I'm in control, He shuts that down real quick…
in a loving parent way though.

He's all these things and more. We could never run out of ways to shout His praises, and though He's all these things, He's still God. And He deserves all that acknowledgement and gratitude for:

- keeping us,
- making a way, and
- lookin' out for us, even when we don't look out for ourselves.

Just like we can use all of these names to call on our God our Father, unfortunately, the food industry has created almost as many names for one ingredient that we're avoiding for the fast: sugar. Even though the focus of the fast isn't on the food, right about now, you're probably feeling a bit of a detox from sugar. Thankfully, you can still have the all-natural kind found in whole fruit juices and dried/fresh fruit, but there are a few other added sugars that are hiding under different names that you should be aware of.

Recently, I read about 56 names for sugar. Some include cane sugar, fructose, and turbinado sugar.

(This is different from the sugars that are in fruits and some vegetables. If it's a whole food, you can have it, so no worries there. We're talking about the fake or animal processed stuff.)

Maybe you do understand why we can't have things like ice-cream, candy or soda. But have you thought about why we can't have things like bread, white flour or white rice? (Or maybe you already know, but still wish it was an option anyway.)

Sugar is literally added to (almost) everything.
Meat...
Bread...

Sugar can also be addicting. Just like Jesus.

" O taste and see that the Lord [our God] is good;
How blessed [fortunate, prosperous, and favored by God] is the man who takes refuge in Him."

- Psalm 34:8 (AMP)

The Lord makes things better when He's in it. He makes us feel lighter, healthier and calm.
Added sugar makes us feel heavier, sicker and cloudy.

To put on the full armor of God like we talked about yesterday, you have to know the forms that the enemy comes in and in our case, it's hidden sugar. When you get a chance, check out my video, "The Many Names of Sugar", about the many kinds of added sugars. That way it'll be easier for you to avoid them.

So, when you are looking at food labels and find one of the many names of sugar, just call on one of the many names of God to carry you through.

Look for ways He is showing out and make a note when it happens. Decide who God will be to you during this fast and write about it here.

Just Rest

Because I'm sure you need to

> *"Come to me, all you who labor and are heavily burdened, and I will give you rest."*
>
> - Matthew 11:28 (WEB)

Raise your hand if you're tired.
Raise your hand if you feel like you have too much to do.
And now raise your hand if you spent time in prayer today.

looks left, looks right

Ok, ok, don't worry, there's likely still time.
And, I'm not here to make you feel bad about yourself.

But I am here to challenge you to do better for yourself. To do that, you have to really think about what's making you tired and taking up your time. It may seem like it's the kids, your job, or your personal life. And yeah, while those are some of the things, it's also (y)our choices. It's the choice to say yes to things that matter and no to things that don't.

I've been reading this devotional called Holy Hustle (in the Bible app) and it talks about focusing on our God given talents to further businesses as well as when to hustle and when to sit down somewhere. (Cuz sometimes that's just what we need to do.)

So while reading it, I decided to check in on a few things to see what's taking up my time and energy. To do this, I decided to use the Screen Time app to see how much time I was spending on different apps on my phone. And below you can find my real stats from the past 6 days. Now mind you, I use my phone for business and some of this includes time spent doing online cooking, but still...

Now, I'm about to put myself on blast and tell you something. At this point, I feel like we're friends in the Spirit, so I know y'all aren't gonna judge me. Right??

Ok, so my results were 5 hours on my phone per day and almost 20% of my time was spent on social media.

Thanfully though since I've been using the app for a few weeks, my social media usage has gone down considerably, and my time on the Bible app, reading, and overall productivity, etc., have gone up as well.

Maybe you're not resting for reasons other than social media. Maybe it's:

- Feeling like you have to have perfectly "put together" kids
- Exhausting yourself trying to keep the house from looking like a tornado came through

When you think about it, rest shouldn't really be optional, but we definitely make it feel like it is. (I know I'm guilty of staying up way past my bedtime.)

Part of the reason we don't rest is because of the to-do list in our heads that seems to go on and on until the end of time. And no matter how much we feel like we get done, there's always more to do.

But it's not always what God has asked us to do...

"Charles Swindoll wrote, "God never asked us to meet life's pressures and demands on our own terms or by relying upon our own strength. Nor did He demand that we win His favor by assembling an impressive portfolio of good deeds. Instead he invites us to enter His rest. God worked and called it good, and He rested and called it Holy."

- Holy Hustle Devotional (Bible App or Book)

And I'm almost 100% certain that you're in that same boat with me feeling this way. So, I've also decided to say no to things, and I'm inviting you to say no too. Say no to feeling like you, your home, and your kids all have to be perfect.

Cuz they won't be.
And that's ok.

But through Christ, we are shown grace, forgiveness, and mercy. So as the laundry goes unfolded or someone's school from goes unsigned, give yourself that same, grace, forgiveness, and mercy.
And give yourself some rest.

So today, I invite you to find rest in Him and through this fast, **focus on what He wants you to focus on.**

Focus on eating through sacrifice and taking time today to hear what He asks you to do in your day to day life. What is God asking you to focus on?

What About Eating Out

Like most folks on the weekend, you're probably thinking about how you can go out and still stay on the fast. You have more options than you realize. Here's how:

- Choose restaurants with build your own options (Ex. Chipotle, Jason's Deli).
- Ask for no cheese/dairy, baked instead of fried, and avoid any cream sauce.
- Tell the restaurant you're vegan and avoiding processed foods.

Eating at a friend's house? Stay on track with these ideas:
- Ask them if there's anything that's dairy and animal free.
- Make an extra batch of a recipe from the week (and take an extra serving with you).
- Eat before you go.

When you're out with others, keep in mind that they'll probably ask why you're eating differently. Use this as a chance to share the point behind the fast.

" But you, when you fast, anoint your head and wash your face, so that you are not seen by men to be fasting, but by your Father who is in secret; and your Father, who sees in secret, will reward you."

- Matthew 6:17-18 (WEB)

Use this scripture as a reminder that even though you feel like the struggle is real, this time is a way to magnify our faith and believe that God will show up as a result of our sacrifice.

What has been the hardest part of the fast so far? The best part?

WEEK 01

Reflection

This week, I saw God show up

_____
_____
_____
_____
_____

One win that I had this week was

_____
_____
_____
_____
_____

This week, I struggled with

_____
_____
_____
_____
_____

I stayed motivated by

_____
_____
_____
_____
_____

WEEK 02

Meal Planner

Each week, use this sheet to plan out your meals, or record what you ate after each meal. Since you'll need your energy, try to eat breakfast each day. Remember to visit www.ChefAshleyShep.com/DanielFastExtras for recipe ideas from my Daniel Fast Pinterest board and the Facebook group.

USE THE KEY TO RECORD YOUR MEALS:
B - BREAKFAST L - LUNCH D - DINNER S - SNACKS

SUN

B _____

L _____

D _____

S _____

MON

B _____

L _____

D _____

S _____

TUES

B _____

L _____

D _____

S _____

WED

B _____

L _____

D _____

S _____

THURS

B _____

L _____

D _____

S _____

FRI

B _____

L _____

D _____

S _____

SAT

B _____

L _____

D _____

S _____

— WEEK 2 —

Scriptures to Reflect Upon:

*"Trust in Yahweh (God) with all your heart,
and don't lean on your own understanding."*
- Proverbs 3:5 (WEB)

---

*"For where your treasure is, there your heart your
wishes, your desires; that on which your life centers
will be also."*
Matthew 6:21 (AMP)

---

*"And when you fast, don't put on a sad face like
the hypocrities. They distort their faces so people will
know they are fasting. I assure you that they have
their reward. When you fast, brush your hair and wash your face.
Then you won't look like you are fasting to people,
but only to your Father who is present in that secret place. Your
Father who sees in secret will reward you. "*
- Matthew 6:16-18 (CEB)

Celebrate
Week 1 Is Done

It's time to celebrate that you've made it through the first week of the Daniel Fast!

Maybe you're thinking that's not much to celebrate. Take a moment to look back at the week and think about:

- All the things you said "no" to that allowed you to say "yes" to God.
- The temptation that you overcame.
- The intentional time that you spent with the Lord.

All of those things are worthy of acknowledgement and celebration.

Maybe the first thing that comes to your mind when you look back over the week isn't celebration. Maybe it's replaying all the times you:

- Forgot to read your devotional.
- Ate something "not allowed" on the fast.
- Focused on how you missed eating a certain food.
- Skipped a few days of journaling.

All of that's okay as well.

I invite you to forgive yourself, and keep it moving. It's natural for us to magnify our failures instead of focusing on what we've done right. However, when we do that, it's like a slap in the face of God.

Jesus died for us so that we could live a life of abundance, joy, and peace. There's no condemnation in Him, so we can't continue to let our minds make us feel less than.

He left it at the cross, so why are you pickin' it up?

Today, write down how you're feeling at the end of week one. Then write your thoughts going into week 2. Take a moment to celebrate what worked and ask for forgiveness for where you messed up. Lastly, forgive yourself.

What do you need to forgive yourself for? How can you start today?

Commit
Commit to Yourself,
Commit to the Lord

During the Daniel Fast, you've taken the time to sacrifice and to commit. After a week in, your eating and praying behaviors are probably starting to set. Behaviors turn into habits, and habits turn into commitment.

Commitment takes:
- Direction
- Focus
- Reinforcement

Luckily, you know someone who can help with all three of those.

> *"Commit your way to Yahweh.*
> *Trust also in him, and he will do this: he will*
> *make your righteousness shine out like light,*
> *and your justice as the noon day sun".*
>
> - Psalm 37:5-6 (WEB)

When you commit yourself to the Lord, He meets you where you are. Here are some ways you can show God that you're committed to growing on purpose.

- Make reading the devotionals and scriptures a habit each day during your quiet time with the Lord.
- Think ahead to situations where you will be tempted and make a plan of how to resist (Ex. birthday party, office potluck, etc.).
- Expect great things from God.

The first two on the list, of course, require discipline, but the last one exceeds them both. It takes faith and hope to believe and expect that God will show up in the next 14 or so days. Do you have it or are you just going through the motions? It's easy to set a timer to pray or to pack a lunch for a day at the office, but how do you handle when you have to "faith" it before you make it?

A few years back on our church anniversary, our outreach pastor declared a simple word that I want to share with you.

"If He said He's gonna do it, He's gonna do it."

- Apostle Roble

If God promised you something, He keeps His word. He doesn't:

- Forget.
- Change His Mind.
- Renege.

That's just how AWESOME He is.
He keeps His word to us, even when we don't keep our word to Him.

> *"Blessed be the Lord, who has given rest to His people Israel, in accordance with everything that He promised. Not one word has failed of all His good promise, which He spoke through Moses His servant."*
>
> - 1 Kings 8:56 (AMP)

Some of us have declared in the private Facebook group what we're believing in, and others stand in agreement with them. If you haven't done either yet, I invite you to join the conversation there. There's still time to come into agreement with what God has in store for you this year whether it's during the fast or after you've completed it. Bring your petitions to the Lord and be open to hear from Him.

And remember, God won't bless mess. So, examine yourself and see what things need to be changed or released so you can walk into God's best for you without hesitation, worry, or fear.

Reflect on what you're believing in God for during the fast, and find scriptures that align with the promises of God.

DAY 10

What's Your Why?
When You Remember Your Why, It Makes Everything Else Easier

If you ask my husband, week 2 is the hardest part of the fast. He says it's right about the time he starts to get tired of the foods that he's eating. That's probably because he sticks to the same foods and doesn't stray too much. He's a creature of habit, like many of us.

So, right about now is when I encourage folks to review their why and what. I challenge them to remember why they are fasting and what are they believing in God for?

I know I've asked you this before, but when we make our declaration publicly known, and decree what the Lord has said to us, it holds us accountable. It also helps us to continue to get closer to Him and trust Him. Finally, when we share our visions with others, it gives us an additional opportunity to have shared purpose and for God to meet us.

> *For where two or three have gathered together in My name, I am there in their midst.*
>
> - Matthew 18:20 (ASV)

When I asked this in the private Facebook group, a few folks shared they're believing in:

- Healing for their husband,
- New employment, and
- Discipline in everyday life.

Sharing our faith goals let us check on and encourage each other when we're just not feelin' it. One of the main points of the challenge is to share your thoughts and feelings with each other as you seek to grow individually and also corporately as the body of Christ.

If you've written here before or posted in the group, thank you. If you haven't yet, I encourage you to do so.

I pray that you have discipline, dedication, and determination this week and next. What's your why for doing this fast? What keeps you going when you want to quit? Lastly, ask God to reveal what's holding you back from fully receiving from Him during this time.

Can vs. Can't
Focus on what you CAN eat

Right about now, your energy might be low. Or maybe you've made a list of all the things you're gonna have once you get off the fast, cuz you can't have them now.

But I invite you to think about all the things you can have.

Now, there are a few different versions of the Daniel Fast depending upon which source you use. But as a general rule, most exclude meat and all animal products (dairy, honey, butter, etc.). Some people feel like those are the best parts of food. My husband Marshall is one of those people lol. Here's what he said about our dinner the other night: "This would be great with some meat in it."

Anyone else or their husband feel this way?

Someone from the Facebook group messaged me to say her husband said the same thing. I suggested a recipe to help him forget about not having meat. Her response was that he'll still think about it regardless.

And mine will/does too. I figure you or your spouse might be feeling the same way.

So my advice is:

Stop looking for what's not there.

Don't look for the meat. Or cheese.
Or sweets.
Cuz they're not there.
That's not why we're here.
And you have to be ok with that.

Instead, realize that you're capable of enduring this. You have already finished a week, and you're not alone in this. You've got me, the group, and most importantly, you've got God.

Most likely you've heard this verse before and are familiar with it. But do you believe it when you're:
- Missing out on that restaurant bread & butter?
- Craving your weekly sweet treat? (ice cream with Reese's + peanut butter for me)
- Skipping out on an extra 15-30 min of social media/tv (so you can have quiet time)?

The more you focus on what you can control and what you can have, the more you can focus on who our help comes from. So, stop focusing on what you can't have, and start focusing on what God can do.

If you need some help, be sure to check out the Bible verses on the extras page to keep you fed physically and spiritually (visit www.ChefAshleyShep.com/DanielFastExtras for more details).

Today, write down what brings you happiness, and find other scriptures that can help you to stay strong during this time.

Which Side Are You on?

At our church, we blend songs together so much that, at times, I'm thinkin' to myself, "Is this even a real song, or did they just come up with this right now?". Either way, one day they played a song that repeats,

"Which side are you on? I'm on the winning side."

I'm not really sure where this song came from, but I am sure that the words are true. One of our worship leaders at church, who leads the song, faced multiple family deaths in the past few months and was on the kidney transplant list for 5 years. One thing that strikes me about him is how consistent he is in encouraging others to join in and worship, even when it looks like the odds are stacked against us. Out of anybody, he would know what that feels like.

But you know, that's what faith is: looking past your current circumstance to believe that God has something for you, and that it will come to pass. It's also knowing that even when the world says you're "losing", God says you're winning.

According to my pastor, Jasper Williams, III, faith is:

- Seeing Something
- Doing Something
- Knowing Something
- Believing Something

> *"Now faith is assurance of things hoped for, proof of things not seen."*
>
> - Hebrews 11:1 (WEB)

The worship leader got a transplant not too long ago, and he's getting stronger each day. While he waited in faith, he decided to praise the Lord along the way. He waited, praised and mourned all together.

But, he knows that God has him in the palm of His hand, keeping and protecting him and his mind.

And you know what? He'll do the same thing for you and me too, because that's just how much He loves us.

So today, I invite you to move your feelings, hunger, and impatience out of the way, and trust God during your battle. Ask yourself:

"Are you gonna stay in your feelings and go back to what's failing? Or are you going to put your faith over what you feel?" -Jasper Williams, III

What major battle are you fighting, and what faith will you need to use to conquer this battle?
What scriptures will keep you motivated during these battles? (Start with the one below)

> *"Having the eyes of your hearts enlightened, that you may know what is the hope of his calling, and what are the riches of the glory of his inheritance in the saints, and what is the exceeding greatness of his power toward us who believe, according to that working of the strength of his might"*
>
> - Ephesians 1:18-19 (WEB)

And remember, with God, you're on the winning side. (Even when it looks like you're losing.)

Jesus Is My Help

Two entries back, I asked you to "stop focusing on what you can't have and start focusing on what our God can do."

The more you focus on what you can control and what you can have, the more you can focus on who our help comes from.

Funny enough, one of my favorite old school gospel songs about this same topic came on tonight while I was writing. It's a pretty simple song with not too many words, but every time it comes on, I jam.

Jam like it's a song that still comes on the radio, because it's just that good. Some of the lyrics say that we have no reason to worry because of all the ways that God has made for us. It also talks about how He has kept His promises.

You can see a full performance of the song - choir robe action and all. Check it out on the extras page.

Anyway, back to the point: Jesus is our help:
- Whether you're fasting or not.
- When you're trapped in a meeting that should've been an email.
- When you're gonna lose it in traffic.

He gives us peace and calms our worried minds, because our futures have already been predestined. He offers the help/guidance/serenity, but it's up to us to follow through and believe it.

He didn't die on the cross for us to take His blood lightly. He came to carry our burdens.

Jesus is my help. And He's your help too.

Write down three things that the Holy Spirit is telling you to leave at the cross during this fast. Since life and death are in the power of the tongue, when you feel yourself falling into old habits or worrying about what you already left at the altar, speak against it. Thank God for the lessons you learned, and let it go.

DAY 14

Countdown
Two Weeks Down
Can you believe that you are almost done with the Daniel Fast?

Some of y'all are like, praises be to God that it's almost over lol.

Others of you are like, wow can't believe it's been 2 weeks already.

Whichever side you're on, I wanted to share a little encouragement during this last week to help you finish strong. I'm always thankful to those who share how the fast has helped and encouraged them. One participant Kim said the following:

"Your devotionals have been so encouraging! Thanks for being obedient to God and living out your purpose. It really has a huge impact on the rest of us."

When I first started writing the devotionals, I had a lot of self doubt about whether I was "qualified" enough to even be leading this. I'll talk more about that on another entry, but though I had that doubting voice in my head, I decided to ignore it and do it anyway. I did it scared... I worried about if someone would "find out" that I didn't "know enough" or wasn't "trained enough" to be able to lead others on this journey. Sometimes in life, we spend so much time worrying about if we have enough of this or enough of that to be able to do things that God tells us we should be doing. If I would have listened to that voice, this journal would still be an idea, and people like Kim would still be looking for encouragement during their Daniel Fast. So, I'm asking you today, in what area of your life are you holding yourself back from what God is telling you to do?

Also, take time today to reflect on your journaling over the past two weeks. Think about how you've transformed in just 14 days.

Have your cravings decreased?
Are you more aware of the foods
you are eating?
Have you made spending time with God a priority
in your day to day life?
Are you kinder or more patient with
yourself or others?
Are you more willing to step out on faith?

If you answered "no" to any of these, it's ok. There's still time to have a breakthrough. Remember God's time is not our time. His ways are not our ways. So stay consistent, and finish strong. He's given you everything you need to endure.

Regardless of how you're feeling, just know that God is pleased with your commitment, and He makes good on His promises. Ask Him if there's an area of your life where your fear is holding you or others back.

WEEK 02

Reflection

This week, I saw God show up

_____

_____

_____

_____

_____

One win that I had this week was

_____

_____

_____

_____

_____

This week, I struggled with

_____

_____

_____

_____

I stayed motivated by

_____

_____

_____

_____

WEEK
08
Meal Planner

Each week, use this sheet to plan out your meals, or record what you ate after each meal. Since you'll need your energy, try to eat breakfast each day. Remember to visit www.ChefAshleyShep.com/DanielFastExtras for recipe ideas from my Daniel Fast Pinterest board and the Facebook group.

USE THE KEY TO RECORD YOUR MEALS:
B - BREAKFAST L - LUNCH D - DINNER S - SNACKS

SUN

B _____

L _____

D _____

S _____

MON

B _____

L _____

D _____

S _____

TUES

B _____

L _____

D_____

S _____

WED

B _____

L _____

D_____

S _____

THURS

B _____

L _____

D_____

S _____

FRI

B _____

L _____

D _____

S _____

SAT

B _____

L _____

D _____

S _____

Scriptures to Reflect Upon:

"Put on the whole armor of God, that you may be able to stand against the wiles of the devil. For our wrestling is not against flesh and blood, but against the principalities, against the powers, against the world's rulers of the darkness of this age, and against the spiritual forces of wickedness in the heavenly places. Therefore put on the whole armor of God, that you may be able to withstand in the evil day, and having done all, to stand.Stand therefore, having the utility belt of truth buckled around your waist, and having put on the breastplate of righteousness, and having fitted your feet with the preparation of the Good News of peace, above all, taking up the shield of faith, with which you will be able to quench all the fiery darts of the evil one. And take the helmet of salvation, and the sword of the Spirit, which is the word of God;"
- Ephesians 6:11-17 (WEB)

"But he answered, It is written, 'Man shall not live by bread alone, but by every word that proceeds out of God's mouth."
- Matthew 4:4 (WEB)

What To Do When You Have Cravings

They're bound to happen sooner or later.

By now, you've probably experienced a craving...or two...or ten. Or maybe you find yourself starving 10 minutes after you had breakfast and wonder how you're gonna make it to lunch, let alone through the rest of the day.

Since this can happen on a regular day when you're not fasting, there's a good chance it's also happened multiple times over the past two weeks. This could be for a lot of different reasons.

- Craving something cuz you're bored
- Craving something cuz you're using it to deal with your feelings (sadness, anger, or whatever other emotion).
- Or maybe if you're like me and your cravings hit you out of habit (ice cream on Friday after work tradition)
- Maybe you're not eating enough during meals and you're actually hungry.

If your cravings are because of the first three reasons, then this is the perfect time to address them and turn them over to the Father. All too often we place our satisfaction in food. Then when it's not as good as we wished it was, we're left craving the next thing to fill that longing. For me, this feeling comes up with dessert.

I'm coming out of this by realizing that my source of fulfilment can't come from chopped up Reese's and peanut butter sauce or even warm apple cinnamon desserts (which I love just as much). It has to come from above. Just like God is our help, He's also our safe place. Even when it comes to food.

> *God is our refuge and strength, a very*
> *present help in trouble.*
>
> - Psalm 46:1 (KJV)

God made the earth and all the fullness thereof (including food) and He created us to require food to maintain us, but not to fulfill us. It's something we have to have everyday, but it's not

something that He wanted us to use as our emotional support, refuge or anything else that takes His place. Hopefully, during this fast, you have seen how food may have crept into that spot for you.

I'm not saying He doesn't want us to enjoy food, because if He didn't, we wouldn't have things like smoked paprika (my favorite seasoning), bacon, or ice cream. But I am saying that He doesn't want our desire for food to be stronger than our desire for Him.

> **Remember, the point of this challenge is to take worrying about food off the table so you have time to focus on God. So, if you're having cravings because you need more food (for your brain to think straight) then of course, I got you covered in the Extras page.**

Make sure you're choosing options that have plenty of plant-based protein like almonds, walnuts, black beans, flax seeds, edamame, etc. And there's a Pinterest board full of approved snack/dessert options if you're working on fighting cravings.

Write how you've replaced your desire for food with your desire for God. If you're not quite there yet, then write about that instead.

Mistakes Happen

On Fridays, in my house, the kitchen is closed.

I need a break, and we like to try new foods outside the house.
So this past Friday, we ordered Thai and Chinese from our local spot.
I almost got the spicy Thai fried rice but figured I shouldn't since it's technically still fried. So brown rice with sautéed veggies it was with some Hot and Sour soup.

After I had a spoonful of soup, my husband, Marshall, asked, *"Can you have that soup?"*

Me: *Yeah, it's just mushrooms, tofu and broth.*

Marsh: *So there's no animal ingredients in there?*

(Beginning to question myself)

Me: *I don't think I used any when I made it last time...*

Searches for recipe
Closes soup container

But isn't that just like life?

Just when you think you've crossed every T and dotted every I, then something turns up out of place, missing or completely forgotten.

Instead of going into the mental space of judging how dumb that was or thinking that God somehow would be upset with me over that, I just put it in the freezer and moved on. I have recently come to the conclusion that this is just yet another sign that I don't have it all together, and I'm not in control.
And that's ok.

I'm not about to let egg ribbons in soup make me feel less than.

I don't have to be perfect, because God is.

I'm an heir to the throne, so my transgressions, mistakes, and human self are completely and totally covered by the redemptive and healing power of the blood of Jesus Christ.

Guess what? The same covering applies to you too.

Now, I also realize the difference between a mistake and a choice. If I would have gotten the fried rice (which I almost did) or decided not to look up the recipe, that would have been a choice that I knew good and well that I didn't need to make.

(And honestly, if I was gonna intentionally break the fast, it would need to be for something like ice cream with Reese's in a waffle bowl. *Any guesses as to what my first dessert off the fast is gonna be?* lol)

Back to the point...

When you make an unintentional mistake whether it be accidentally consuming something not on the fast or snapping on someone, because you're hangry (hungry + angry), make the choice to ask for forgiveness from God. Then actually forgive yourself.

Often we're our harshest critics, partially because we:

- Can't get out of our own heads, and/or
- Set such high and often unattainable standards for ourselves.

And sometimes those aren't even standards God has set out for us to meet. (That's another devotional for another day.)

So today, take a moment to write down 3 areas of your life that you need to give yourself some grace on.
Then make the decision to actually forgive yourself...because the Father already has.

Did God Ask You To Do That?

So, about that to do list...

Yesterday we talked about how we all make mistakes and that if we ask for forgiveness then we are forgiven...right then and there. And on Day 6, we talked about resting. Sometimes we put so much pressure on ourselves to:

- Do "all the things,"
- Follow expectations set by others, and/or
- Live up to what we see others doing.

None of that is of God.

Recently, I was listening to a podcast about the book, *The One Thing*. It focuses on the question: "What's the one thing that you need to do to make everything else easier?" In the book, the authors address our never-ending to do list. They also talk about how we can change that list to a success list by focusing on the 3-5 activities that really matter the most. They suggest asking ourselves these things to figure out that one thing:

*"What's the one thing on my list that if I could do today that will give the greatest return
towards my goals?
What will make the rest of my week easier?
What's the most impactful? "*

- Jay Papasan

I liked their list from an organizational standpoint, but I want to add a few other questions.

- What will bring glory to the Kingdom of God?
- What will give me more energy for the week to share with my family or myself?
- Is this God's plan for my life or someone else's?

And finally...

Did God tell me to do that?

> *"If then you were raised together with Christ, seek the things that are above, where Christ is, seated on the right hand of God. Set your mind on the things that are above, not on the things that are on the earth."*
>
> - Colossians 3:1-2 (WEB)

And there are three things that will definitely fit on that list:
1. Prayers
2. Praising God
3. Preparing Meals

Each of those things will give you a clear focus and purpose for the week. Get anchored and be ready.

If you haven't already, take some time today to first honor God. Then honor yourself by either checking out the recipes, meal plans, and grocery shopping lists on the Extras page, so you can spend time focusing on the other things on your success list.

We have to stop filling our lives with things that keep us busy and start filling it with things that keep us purposeful.

Identify three tasks that are the most important focus, and then select the one thing that you'll work on for this week. When you're done, share in the private Facebook group. You never know who you might motivate.

Do You Miss It?

The soda, the fries, and the cookies...

A few days back, I mentioned that ice cream with Reese's would be my first dessert after the fast. But, I don't even really crave it all that much anymore.

> *"So whether you eat or drink whatever you do, do it all or the glory of God."*
>
> - 1 Corinthians 10:31

Honestly, it doesn't hold as big of a place in my heart or stomach anymore.

Or maybe it's because I've had to manage my stress/emotions in ways that didn't involve food? When we look to food to make us complete, here's what happens:
We...

- Get excited.
- Eat the food.
- Search for the next thing that will fill the gap of happiness again.

Growing up, each year, there'd always be that one special Barbie that I wanted with long hair or the designer convertible. My collection grew for years which led to hours of fun only to decide around age 11 that I'd be happy to give the entire thing to a 6-year-old little girl.

I didn't want them, because they no longer served their purpose. So, I simply moved on. Too often we do this with food: we get it, become uninterested when we have it, and move on to the next to fill a bottomless hole. I've realized that now that I'm around food more often for my job, I think about it more, and find ways to excuse these thoughts as research or work.

Don't miss the message. I'm still gettin' my ice cream at some point once the fast is over. I'm sure that God is ok with that. He knows the desires of my heart. LOL

BUT He also knows that He's my source of long term happiness or joy and not food. Food can be my happiness, but never my joy. I've had far too many meals that didn't live up to expectations to be placing my peace and joy in things controlled by man. So, I'm becoming more in tune with the reasons why I'm reaching for that ice cream/those chips/ etc. Is it because I'm:

Bored?

Worried?

Used to having it every Friday?

Once it's had, it's almost as if it's out of sight, out of mind, and I'm on to the next menu item to fill that same longing for the newest, tastiest thing. (I know I'm not alone.)

Even worse, we do the same thing with God.

We look to Him to deliver us from a situation and celebrate that He brought us out, and then allow petty things that are happening in our daily lives to upset us and steal our happiness. It brings us right back to where we were before we reached out to Him. Then we don't remember the last time He made a way.

Just like food shouldn't be our joy, we shouldn't let life's circumstances steal our joy. We know how the story ends and it's with us being protected and covered by the Father.

Here are a few verses to help you to remember that.

> *"Rejoic[e] in hope; [be] patient in tribulation; continu[e] steadfastly in prayer;"*
>
> - Romans 12:12 (ASV)

> *"A cheerful heart is good medicine; But a broken spirit drieth up the bones..."*
>
> - Proverbs 17:22 (ASV)

So when you finish the fast, enjoy the food, and let it make you happy. But remember that your joy lies with the Lord. Is there a food that you no longer crave since being on the fast? How do you feel differently?

Decisions, Decisions

In a few days, the fast will be over, and I'm handing your meal planning back over to you.

BUT you don't have to go it alone.
I have a couple of options that I want to remind you of, so here's a quick run down:

Whatever you decide to do, know that you've got options. All of these resources are available at
www.ChefAshleyShep.com/DanielFastExtras

- Wanna stick to a plant based diet?   (Vegan)--> Check out the Dope Meal Planner.
- Need to know what's for dinner ahead of time? Check out Plan to Eat.
- Don't know what you need, but know you need help? Pick a time to chat with me for a free consultation call to help you simplify meal time™.
- Want to have meals ready for weeks? Check out my Make Ahead Meals Masterclass.

Now that you have some options, let's get back to business. Everybody loves to quote Habakkuk 2:2, Write the vision and make it plain. But then folks still:

- Struggle when it comes to dinner time,
- Buy a bag of chopped lettuce to throw out when it's still unopened a few days later, and
- Go grocery shopping while hungry, because there was no vision and no plan. Valuable time, money, and energy gets wasted, when it all could have been used to further God's kingdom or take a minute to breathe.

Of course, this doesn't just apply to food. Consider ways that lack of planning or tapping into God's vision for your life has affected you negatively. Insert whatever thing that's taking up too much of your time & energy.

In order to receive God's best for us, it's our job to be available mentally, spiritually, and physically. And sis, if you're scrambling with the day to day issues of life, there's no way you're going to have the mental energy, let alone time, to complete your assignment.

Your assignment could be:

- Having a strong marital foundation to build a life for the next generation,
- Raising successful well-informed little humans, and/or
- Excelling at your career and making room at the table for others.

Whatever your assignment is, I promise that you won't get there letting things like dinner stress you out every day or by eating take out multiple days a week. God's vision for our lives is to find ways to honor Him in all that we do. So I want to ask you:

Are you honoring God in your relationships with your health or on your job?
Honestly, probably not as much as you could be. Take the time right now (90 seconds or less) and write down:

1. What's one way you can honor God in your relationships?
2. What's one way you can honor God in your prayer life?
3. What's one way you can honor God in your professional life?

For today, write about how you're going to make more room in your life for God's vision.

*"Where there is no vision,
the people will perish."*

- Proverbs 29:18 (KJV)

Proclaim God's vision over your life.

You're Qualified

Can I let you in on a secret? At the time of hosting my first Daniel Fast 21 Day Food and Faith Challenge, I had only completed the fast once.

Crazy right?

To say that developing the challenge (where these devotionals came from) has been an amazing experience is an understatement. Hearing from challenge participants about how it impacted them warms my heart. This is what the folks have had to say:

"It has taken me a few days to respond because I was talked into doing this by a friend. I had never heard of (the) Daniel Fast. I wasn't really sure what I was doing this for. Well, after the horrible migraine for two days, feeling like I was starving, as of today, 5 days in I feel like this is (the) best thing I have ever done. I want my spirit to keep growing in Christ. I want to be able to lay my burdens down and have faith God has already taken care of them. I want to be more obedient and not get in the way of my blessings....I'm believing in God to feed my spirit and soul as I starve my flesh from its unhealthy living. Thank you for the great recipes. God bless..."

"Thank you so much. You're definitely helping things go smoother this time around. Last year I was so miserable and barely ate."

"This blessed me so much today".

And if this journal has been a blessing to you, please take the survey
to share your thoughts or leave a review on Amazon here:
www.ChefAshleyShep.com/DanielFastExtras.

Now, this isn't a moment to brag, but it is a moment to talk about how
we can limit what God can do in our lives by being narrow minded or
disobedient. In January 2018, when a friend from church, Liz, shared
how she didn't know what she was going to eat while on the fast, I
could have easily said:
- I wasn't in business long enough (It had only been 6 months).
- I wasn't vegan.
- I had only ever done the Daniel Fast once (before).

Instead, I said that I'll try it out, and because of obedience, the
Daniel Fast 21 Day Food and Faith Challenge was born. Then this
journal was created. It didn't matter how many years I had fasted or
how long I had been in business; I realized that this challenge was
anointed, and food could be my ministry.

God doesn't call the qualified, He qualifies the called. There are tons
of examples in the Bible of real-life people who were messed up, but
God chose them to be the change agents of their generation. Now
we're still talking about them thousands of years later, because they
made the choice to follow God's nudging.

So I'm asking you:

What are you being called to do that you feel unqualified for?
- What blessings are you blocking, because you refuse to believe
  that you're who God says you are?
- How are you holding back from your family and friends, because of
  lack of forgiveness for them (and yourself)?
- How many more people could you bless with the gifts that you
  aren't willing to share?

"Your gift is someone else's struggle. Why would you insult God by hiding your gift and not setting someone else free?"

- Amber L. Wright, Conversation Coach & Speaker

(drops mic)

He knew you before you knew yourself, so why even try to hide?

What are you qualified for but continue to hold back on?

Remember Habakkuk 2:2 and start thinking about your meal time plan for after the fast, because without vision, the people perish.
How is feeling unqualified affecting your vision of yourself or your family?

DAY 21

Congratulations

You made it!
Of course you would, because God's on your side.

They say it takes 21 days to form a habit.

Today is the 21st day where you've fostered healthy habits for your body and spirit. The choice is yours to continue on this path or to return to your old ways.

The hubby and I were talking about what we'd want our first meal off of the fast to be. By now you can tell that desserts are pretty much our thing, so the conversation quickly turned to that. For Marshall, that meant deciding between getting a cinnamon roll or cake from our favorite local bakery. He said he's also ready to have bread back in his life. For me, I wasn't sure what I'd prefer. However, regardless of what I pick, I know that true satisfaction doesn't come from food. It comes from God above, and I hope that's what you've learned too.

I pray that this journey has been one of growth, spiritual stretching, and of faith. God meets us where we are and regardless of if this was your first time or your fifteenth time fasting, He appreciates your intentionality and focus.

I want to thank you again for letting me uplift, support, and encourage you. Continue to find ways to seek Him out in your everyday life, and know that a relationship with Him is better than any food. Today, write about how you feel on this final day of the fast and reflect upon where God brought you from in such a short amount of time.

Congratulations on completing the Daniel Fast!

Record your thoughts below from the entire experience.

During this fast, I learned that I

During this fast, I learned that God

After the fast, my next steps are

WEEK 08

Reflection

This week, I saw God show up

_____

_____

_____

_____

_____

One win that I had this week was

_____

_____

_____

_____

_____

This week, I struggled with

_____

_____

_____

_____

_____

I stayed motivated by

_____

_____

_____

_____

_____

DAY 22

What Now?

Now that the Daniel Fast is over for you, have you thought about:

- What you're going to eat once the fast is over?
- How are you going to continue to grow in your faith?

How are you going to use all that you've learned now that you've grown closer to God? If your answer to these questions is "I don't know." then keep reading on to find out.

Reintroduce foods slowly

The day after the fast is not the day to go to a buffet. (Trust me, this will not end well LOL). Your body needs time to adjust back to the foods that you have left out. If you eat meat, start slowly and go easy with things like dairy for the first few days.

Find another devotional or Bible reading plan.

One past participant said "[My favorite part about the Daniel Fast Food and Faith Challenge is] the daily inspiration because it keeps me focused on God and why I'm doing it." There are plenty of options of devotionals between *Jesus Calling* or even the Bible app by Life. Church which is absolutely free. Either option you pick will help keep you on track and make this a lifestyle change. You have to get more word into your spirit to maintain and grow.

Eat mindfully

Did you notice that you had more energy during the fast than you normally do? (This would of course be after the days you were on the struggle bus recovering from your sugar withdrawals.) That's because you were eating more of what your body needs: whole foods from the earth. So when you eat, think about a few things:

- Why am I eating this? (boredom or nourishment)
- Will eating this help me meet my goals? (80% of the time, you need to be saying yes)

Check in with yourself regularly to see if what you're putting into your body aligns with who and what you want to be. Are you honoring God's temple with your eating?

———

Stay Connected

- Like or follow me on Facebook, Instagram, and Pinterest @ChefAshleyShep.
- Visit my website www.ChefAshleyShep.com.
- Join the Food Fam Facebook Group for more ways to simplify meal time™.
- All links can be found on the Daniel Fast Extras page at www. ChefAshleyShep.com/DanielFastExtras.

———

Got opinions?

If you haven't already, be sure to take the survey or leave a review on Amazon to be able to help others experience what you did during this time.

Share with a friend

If you were blessed by this journal, take a second to share with someone who needs to experience this.
Who in your life would benefit from hearing from the Lord like you have over the last 21 days?
For those who prefer that the inspiration come to them, I also offer this journal in the form of a series of daily devotional emails, as a part of the Daniel Fast 21 Day Food and Faith Challenge on the extra resources page
(www.ChefAshleyShep.com/DanielFastExtras).

Finally, don't forget...

During this journey, we talked about many options to help you get dinner done faster such as Plan to Eat, The Dope Vegan Meal Planner, and more. Remember to check out those links on the Extras page as well as some bonuses that you can enjoy as a thank you for your purchase.
Visit www.ChefAshleyShep.com/DanielFastExtras to see them all.
Also, if you need help staying on track with meals, contact me to talk about specific solutions for your family.

Thank you and God bless.

ABOUT THE AUTHOR

Chef Ashley Shep

An educator by trade and personal chef by practice, Chef Ashley Shep decided to take her love of food and teaching to the masses by launching a movement that focuses on simplifying meal time™ , getting dinner done faster, and destroying the myth that food that tastes good can't be good for you. She's on a mission to help busy, working moms across the globe reclaim their time from meal time.

She began her meal prep journey as a way to save time and energy, but ended up finding a calling. Chef Ashley Shep is at your service!

You can connect with Chef Ashley Shep by liking or following on Facebook, Instagram, and Pinterest @ChefAshleyShep.

Also, be sure to visit www.ChefAshleyShep.com/DanielFastExtras for resources connected to this journal and www.ChefAshleyShep.com for more tips and ideas about getting dinner done faster.

NOTES

NOTES

NOTES

Made in the USA
Coppell, TX
19 July 2021